Crossing Midnight
the sword in the soul

Mike Carey
WRITER

Jim Fern
José Villarrubia
Gabriel Hernandez
Mateo Guerrero
J.H. Williams III
ARTISTS

Todd Klein
LETTERER

J.H. Williams III
ORIGINAL SERIES
COVERS

CROSSING MIDNIGHT created by
Mike Carey and Jim Fern

KAREN BERGER
Senior VP-Executive Editor

PORNSAK PICHETSHOTE
Editor-original series

SCOTT NYBAKKEN
Editor-collected edition

ROBBIN BROSTERMAN
Senior Art Director

PAUL LEVITZ
President & Publisher

GEORG BREWER
VP-Design & DC Direct Creative

RICHARD BRUNING
Senior VP-Creative Director

PATRICK CALDON
Executive VP-Finance & Operations

CHRIS CARAMALIS
VP-Finance

JOHN CUNNINGHAM
VP-Marketing

TERRI CUNNINGHAM
VP-Managing Editor

ALISON GILL
VP-Manufacturing

DAVID HYDE
VP-Publicity

HANK KANALZ
VP-General Manager, WildStorm

JIM LEE
Editorial Director-WildStorm

PAULA LOWITT
Senior VP-Business & Legal Affairs

MARYELLEN McLAUGHLIN
VP-Advertising & Custom Publishing

JOHN NEE
Senior VP-Business Development

GREGORY NOVECK
Senior VP-Creative Affairs

SUE POHJA
VP-Book Trade Sales

STEVE ROTTERDAM
Senior VP-Sales & Marketing

CHERYL RUBIN
Senior VP-Brand Management

JEFF TROJAN
VP-Business Development, DC Direct

BOB WAYNE
VP-Sales

Cover illustration by J. H. Williams III
Logo design by Glenn Parsons of Astrolux Design
Publication design by Amelia Grohman

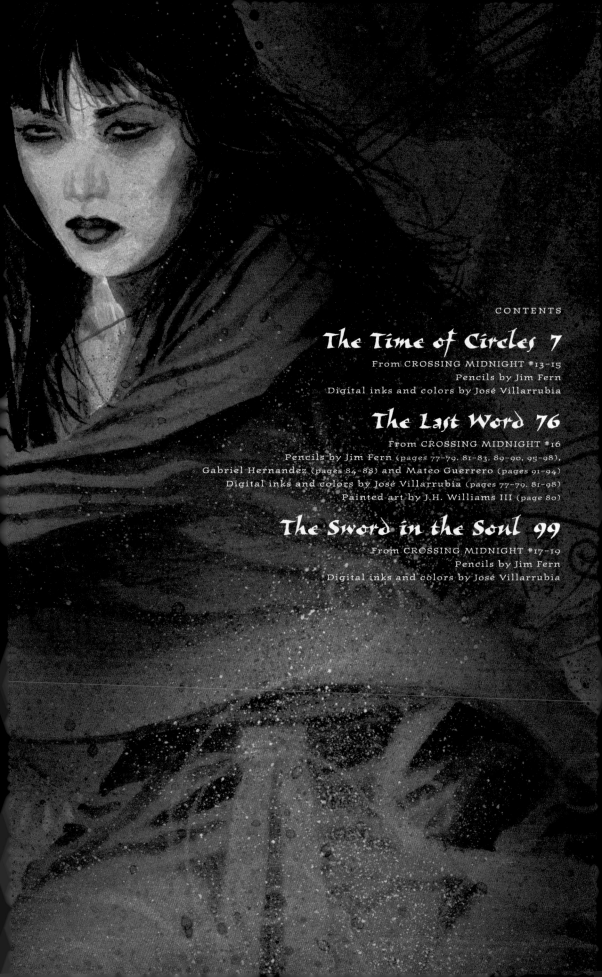

CONTENTS

The Time of Circles 7

From CROSSING MIDNIGHT #13-15
Pencils by Jim Fern
Digital inks and colors by José Villarrubia

The Last Word 76

From CROSSING MIDNIGHT #16
Pencils by Jim Fern (pages 77-79, 81-83, 89-90, 95-98),
Gabriel Hernandez (pages 84-88) and Mateo Guerrero (pages 91-94)
Digital inks and colors by José Villarrubia (pages 77-79, 81-98)
Painted art by J.H. Williams III (page 80)

The Sword in the Soul 99

From CROSSING MIDNIGHT #17-19
Pencils by Jim Fern
Digital inks and colors by José Villarrubia

CROSSING MIDNIGHT:
The Sword in the Soul

The palace of the SWORD-KING.

Three hours ago.

BY ORDER OF *LORD ARATSU*, YOU WILL FILL IN THESE *REQUISITIONS* WITHOUT DELAY OR QUESTION.

I'VE GOT *WORK* TO DO.

WELL, I'LL DO MY *BEST*, AS ALWAYS. BUT I WONDER WHAT'S MARRED YOUR MANNERS, *HASHARITO.*

AND WHAT A SCRAPE-GRACE COULD *WANT* WITH SUCH STUFF AS THIS.

I'M SORRY, *MUMBU-TAI.* I'M JUST IN A HURRY, THAT'S ALL.

CAN'T CALL YOURSELF *THAT* UNTIL YOU'VE GOT A KILL.

I HAVE A *TARGET.* AN AGENT OF LORD ARATSU'S ENEMIES, WHO HUNTS *ME* IN MY TURN.

HIS NAME IS *KAIKOU HARA*-- AND HE'S A *KONDOBU.*

HEH. IMMUNE TO *MAGICS*, THEN. YOUR LITTLE SCISSORS WON'T HELP YOU MUCH. MAYBE YOU SHOULD LET SOMEONE *ELSE* CLAIM THIS PELT.

AND I'M NOT A SCRAPE-GRACE ANY-MORE.

I'M AN *ASSASSIN.*

NO. HE'S *MINE*. IF HE WANTS TO KILL *ME* TOO, IT'S A FAIR FIGHT.

AND LORD ARATSU HAS PROMISED TO RESTORE MY *MEMORIES* WHEN I BRING BACK THIS BOY'S HEAD.

ANYWAY, ONE NIGHT OF GRUBBING IN PEOPLE'S *DREAMS* AND BEING SNEERED AT BY THE STREET YOKAI WAS *ENOUGH*.

I KNOW I CAN BE *MORE*. I KNOW I WAS *MEANT* TO BE MORE.

KAIKOU HARA'S *DEATH* IS MY DOORWAY.

I'LL DO WHATEVER IT *TAKES* TO BRING HIM TO IT.

THE TIME OF CIRCLES

The sword-king's private quarters.

Ninety minutes ago.

AH, GOOD. YOU'RE THE NEW ONE. COME IN, KISHIMO--

KISHIMO--?

KISHIMO-SAI, MY LORD ARATSU. YOU ASKED TO BE INFORMED WHEN HASHARITO LEFT ON HER MISSION.

YES, I DID. BUT I KNOW SHE'S GONE. I FELT HER LEAVE.

THE WORLD ROCKS IN HER WAKE LIKE AN UNBALLASTED BOAT.

SHE IS WONDERFUL, IS SHE NOT? ONE NIGHT! SHE FACES DOWN THE GLEANER AND LIVES.

SHE REBELS AGAINST THE ROLE I'VE ASSIGNED HER...

SHE HAS POWER IN HER, MY LORD, THAT'S TRUE. A GREATNESS. IN TRUTH, SHE REMINDS ME OF--

...

OF WHAT?

OF NOTHING, MY LORD. OF NOBODY.

The Hara family apartment, Nagasaki.

Now.

PRRRRRRT
PRRRRRRT

YES?

HELLO, MOM. IT'S ME.

KAI! KAIKOU!

OH, I'VE BEEN SO WORRIED ABOUT YOU! WHERE ARE YOU? ARE YOU ALL RIGHT?

I'M FINE. I'M STILL IN TOKYO.

AND I'VE FOUND SOMEONE WHO KNOWS TOSHI. SOMEONE WHO'S SEEN HER.

YOU HAVE? THAT'S--THAT'S WONDERFUL!

WHAT'S WONDERFUL? HAS HE FOUND HER?

AND ASK HIM WHERE HE'S STAYING!

WELL, I HAVEN'T TALKED TO THIS WOMAN YET. IT MIGHT NOT COME TO ANYTHING.

HER NAME IS MIMI. SHE SAYS SHE'S TOSHI'S FRIEND.

SOMEONE'S **SEEN** HER.

IN TOKYO?

YES, IN TOKYO. KAI, YOUR FATHER WANTS TO KNOW WHERE YOU **ARE.**

I'M STAYING IN A **HOTEL.**

A **DECENT** ONE? SOME-WHERE SAFE AND CENTRAL?

YEAH, I-- YEAH. DEFINITELY. A REALLY NICE PLACE.

CAN YOU GIVE US THE ADDRESS? WE DON'T WANT TO LOSE **TOUCH** WITH YOU AGAIN.

1370 DEBA STREET. IN CHIYODA. ROOM 2616.

KAI, WE'RE GOING TO COME AND JOIN YOU. YOU'RE TOO **YOUNG** TO BE--

≹CLICK≹

HE HUNG UP.

YOU SHOULD HAVE LET **ME** TALK TO HIM.

I DIDN'T GET THE **CHANCE,** YASUO. HE JUST--

WE'RE ON OUR WAY, SUPERDOG.

WE'RE ON OUR **WAY.**

THANKS, LORETTA.

NO CHARGE, COUNTRY BOY. YOU CAN JUST BE MY *SEX-SLAVE* FOR A DAY.

HOW COME YOU HUNG *UP* ON THEM? SEEMED KIND OF *COLD*.

THERE'S JUST TOO MUCH I CAN'T *EXPLAIN*. ABOUT WHAT I'M DOING HERE. WHAT'S BEEN HAPPENING.

AND MY MOM WILL *KNOW* IF I LIE TO HER. IT'S BETTER TO SAY NOTHING--UNTIL I BRING TOSHI *HOME*.

SPEAKING OF HOME-- I'VE GOT TO GO. EVEN MY FOLKS MIGHT NOTICE IF I STAY AWAY FOR TWO DAYS STRAIGHT. WHEN DO YOU SEE THE *BEGGAR* LADY?

I GUESS I'LL GO THERE IN THE MORNING.

COOL. COME AND TELL ME HOW IT *WENT*.

TOMORROW? PROMISE?

TOMORROW.

I--ABSOLUTELY.

TOMORROW--

TOMORROW'S ALREADY *HERE,* BECAUSE IT'S TWO IN THE MORNING.

BUT I WANDER THE STREETS OF CHIBA LIKE A *GHOST,* HOUR AFTER HOUR.

AND GHOSTS *WATCH* ME. I'M ON THEIR WAVE-LENGTH NOW. I'M IN THEIR WORLD.

GHOSTS. MONSTERS. LOST SOULS.

BUT THEY DON'T *INTRUDE* BECAUSE THEY CAN SEE WHAT KIND OF A *MOOD* I'M IN.

OR PERHAPS THEY CAN SMELL THAT THE *BLOOD* ON MY HANDS IS THE BLOOD OF THEIR OWN *KIND.*

THE YALA DAM IS A *COFFIN* HOTEL.

IT'S GOING TO SEEM PRETTY *GRIM* AFTER THE IMPERIAL, BUT IT WAS ALL I COULD *AFFORD.*

ANYWAY, WE COULDN'T GO BACK.

AND I COULDN'T ASK *LORETTA* FOR MONEY NOW THAT I KNOW SHE HUGS MIDDLE-AGED *SARARIMEN* TO GET IT.

SO IT'S *THIS* PLACE OR NOTHING.

CRKKKKKK

AND I MAY SOUND LIKE A COUNTRY *BUMPKIN* WHEN I SAY THIS--

--BUT SUDDENLY *NOTHING* SEEMS LIKE A PRETTY GOOD IDEA.

SUPPOSE I WENT TO UENO PARK *NOW?* IN THE MIDDLE OF THE NIGHT?

2616

WOULD THIS MIMI-SAMA AGREE TO *SEE* ME?

AND HOW CAN SHE *LIVE* IN A PARK ANYWAY? WHAT DOES THAT *MEAN?*

CUBICLE 2616 HAS THREE USED *CONDOMS* LYING RIGHT INSIDE THE DOOR.

2616

I GUESS THE LAST RESIDENT WAS TOO *TIRED* AFTER THE THIRD TIME TO CLEAN UP AFTER HIMSELF.

AND I GUESS I'LL SLEEP *LATER.*

2616

FUNNY PLACE FOR AN *ASSASSIN* TO LIVE, EH, SEN? MAYBE HE'S DOWN ON HIS *LUCK.*

OR MAYBE HE *LIKES* TO--

...

≥snf! snf!≥

2616

TIME TO EARN YOUR *KEEP,* SUPERDOG.

2616

KAIKOU HARA.

I HOPE IT'S NOT TOO *LATE.* STONE-FIST SAID YOU WANTED TO SEE ME, SO I--

EXTREME LOVE!!!

--I THOUGHT-- ...

切恋愛
EXTREME LOVE!!!

STARRING MIMI OGUNO

Y-YOU-- --YOU'RE-- --YOU'RE *MIMI OGUNO.*

YES, I AM. YOU'VE SEEN SOME OF MY *FILMS?*

I--I SAW *INSATIABLE NURSES* AT MY FRIEND'S HOUSE. LOTS OF--LOTS OF TIMES.

UNTIL THE *TAPE* BROKE.

THEN THERE DOESN'T NEED TO BE ANY CEREMONY OR *STIFFNESS* BETWEEN US, KAIKOU.

WE'RE *INTIMATE* ALREADY.

MY INSTINCT IS TO TRUST YOU. I'M USED TO *FOLLOWING* MY INSTINCTS.

AND ANY *FOOL* COULD SEE THAT YOUR SISTER IS UNHAPPY.

THEN SHE *WAS* HERE?

YES. SHE WAS HERE. SHE HELPED ME WITH A--*PERSONAL* PROBLEM.

AND THEN SHE LEFT BEFORE I COULD PROPERLY *THANK* HER.

DO YOU KNOW WHERE SHE *WENT?*

NO. BUT SHE'S A *SCRAPE-GRACE,* AS *I* WAS WHEN I WAS HER AGE.

THAT MEANS SHE'S IN THE SERVICE OF *ASIROSAMIRO,* THE SWORD-KING.

YOU MEAN *ARATSU?*

GOOD GRACIOUS, NO. ARATSU IS ONLY A JUMPED-UP *SERVING MAN.* I MEAN THE KNIFE-KAMI HIMSELF.

SO IF YOU WANT TO SEE YOUR *SISTER* AGAIN--

--YOU'LL HAVE TO GO TO HIS *HOUSE.*

IT WAS ANOTHER *LIFE.* A LONG TIME AGO, NOW. IT'S STRANGE HOW YOUR LIFE FORMS IN *LAYERS.* LIKE SNOW FALLING.

THE KAMI REALM IS A DANGEROUS PLACE, KAI. BUT THE SWORD-KING IS *HONORABLE.* HE'LL GIVE YOU A STRAIGHT ANSWER. YES OR NO.

MIMI, I THINK IT'S POSSIBLE THAT THINGS HAVE *CHANGED* SINCE YOU LAST...DID THIS STUFF.

THAT PLACE *DOESN'T* CHANGE. IT'S LIKE A CLIFF BY THE SEA.

OUR WORLD *BREAKS* AGAINST IT AND SHATTERS. AGAIN AND AGAIN AND AGAIN, FOR ALL *TIME.*

MIMI-SAMA, WHERE IS THE *LOCK* THAT YOUR KEY FITS? HOW CAN I GET THROUGH TO WHERE *TOSHI* IS?

THERE *IS* NO LOCK, KAIKOU.

THAT'S NOT HOW IT *WORKS.*

WHEN I WAS A SCRAPE-GRACE, I COULD JUST *THINK* ABOUT MY MASTER'S HOUSE AND I'D *BE* THERE.

BUT NOT ANY- *MORE?*

NO. NOT ANYMORE. HE ONLY ALLOWS HIS *SERVANTS* TO COME AND GO IN THAT WAY.

BUT THERE ARE *GATES.* AND SO LONG AS YOU HOLD THE KEY, THE GATES WILL LET YOU THROUGH.

TO WHERE THE *SWORD-KING* LIVES.

CAN YOU TELL ME WHERE THESE GATES ARE? OR *TAKE* ME TO ONE?

THE NEAREST IS AT THE *NISHIDAI* SUBWAY STATION. THE EASTBOUND TUNNEL ON THE MITA LINE.

STONE-FIST WILL TAKE YOU THERE.

I WAS EXPECTING THE KEY TO BE *COLD* TO THE TOUCH. BUT IT WAS WARM, AND IT *SQUIRMED* IN MY HAND LIKE SOMETHING *ALIVE*.

EVEN AFTER ALL I'D BEEN THROUGH--IT *SCARED* ME.

STAY WITH HIM. KEEP HIM SAFE.

DON'T WORRY, MIMI-SAMA. ANYONE WHO TRIES TO HURT HIM WILL EAT THEIR OWN *TEETH.*

THANK YOU, MIMI-SAMA. THANK YOU FOR EVERYTHING--ESPECIALLY FOR *TRUSTING* ME.

I HOPE I CAN *REPAY* YOU SOME DAY.

COME BACK *ALIVE,* KAIKOU.

AND WATCH *INSATIABLE NURSES II*--IT'S A FAR BETTER MOVIE.

LORETTA!

WHAT ARE YOU *DOING* IN THERE?

I'M BLEACHING MY *EYEBROWS!*

GOD, CAN I GET A *MOMENT'S* PEACE?

YOU'VE BEEN IN THERE FORTY-FIVE *MINUTES!*

WELL, IF THAT'S HOW LONG IT TAKES, THEN THAT'S HOW LONG IT *TAKES.*

I'M NOT RUSHING THE FINAL *RINSE* BECAUSE YOUR BLADDER IS TOO SMALL TO--

HI. YOU MUST BE *LORETTA.* TELL ME ABOUT *KAIKOU HARA.*

WHILE YOUR *HEAD* IS STILL ATTACHED TO YOUR NECK.

HOW DID YOU COME TO *WORK* FOR MIMI-SAMA?

50

SHE KILLED MY *FATHER*.

SHE *WHAT?* SHE-- KILLED--?

RIGHT. AND I DIDN'T HAVE ANY *MONEY* TO PAY HER BACK.

SO I SAID I'D BE A *LEG-BREAKER* FOR HER INSTEAD. IT'S WORKED OUT PRETTY *WELL* SO FAR.

CLACK

YOU'RE SHOCKED.

NO. I'M-- JUST--

MY FAMILY WASN'T LIKE YOURS, KID. IT WAS MORE LIKE--YOU KNOW--ONE OF THOSE *PITS* WHERE THEY MAKE RATS FIGHT DOGS.

I WISH *I'D* HAD A BROTHER LIKE YOU.

I'M THINKING MY DAD WOULD HAVE DIED A LOT *SOONER.*

TSSHRIKK

THE GRASS WAS *WET*, EVEN THOUGH IT HADN'T RAINED.

DEW, MAYBE. OR SPRINKLERS. A LOT OF THE STATIONS HAVE SPRINKLERS THAT COME ON AT NIGHT.

THEY ALSO HAVE BULLET TRAINS THAT COME THROUGH AT 300 MILES AN HOUR.

I WATCHED THE TRACKS. THEY VIBRATE WHEN A TRAIN IS COMING.

BUT THE AIR GENERALLY DOESN'T.

THERE. *THERE*, STONE-FIST.

WHY IS IT *ME* DOING THIS?

BECAUSE THE KEY WON'T *WORK* WHILE I'M TOUCHING IT. NOTHING MAGICAL *DOES*.

HAVE YOU *FOUND* IT?

YEAH. I *THINK* SO.

SHVVVVVVVVVV

MIMI'S SWORD-KING ISN'T THE *SAME* AS THE ONE I MET. THIS MAN--KILLS WITHOUT EVEN *THINKING* ABOUT IT.

AND WE'RE WALKING RIGHT INTO HIS HOUSE. I *HAVE* TO DO THIS. BUT YOU--

FORGET IT, BITE-SIZE. I'M GOING ALL THE WAY.

FIRST TIME I'VE EVER SAID THAT TO A *BOY*, BY THE WAY. YOU SHOULD BE *FLATTERED.*

STAY CLOSE TO THE *GATE* ON THE OTHER SIDE.

WE COULD BE WALKING INTO HIS BEDROOM, HIS DUNGEON, ANYTHING.

WE MIGHT NEED TO BACK OUT *FAST* IF WE SEE ANY KIND OF--

...

BEEN HERE LESS THAN TWO HOURS, AND ALREADY I WANT TO **KILL** SOMEONE.

LOCK MY **THIGHS** ON EITHER SIDE OF THEIR HEAD, FLEX AND **TWIST**.

IT'S BECAUSE OF THE **ISLANDS**.

BECAUSE JAPAN IS LIKE A **BREAD ROLL** BROKEN INTO CRUMBS AND SPRINKLED ON THE **SEA**.

IDZUMI TAISHA?

HAI! DZUMI TAISHA, TSUTSU **MAIRU**. SOKO.

EVERY MILE YOU TRAVEL AWAY FROM TOKYO IS **TEN** MILES-- AND TEN **YEARS**.

SO BY THE TIME YOU GET TO **SHIMANE** PROVINCE YOU'RE RIGHT AT THE EDGE OF THE **WORLD**.

AND BACK IN THE FUCKING **STONE AGE**.

OR MAYBE IT'S BECAUSE OF THE **KID**.

I MEAN, ONE OF THE **ADVANTAGES** OF THE DYKE LIFESTYLE IS THAT YOU DON'T HAVE TO **DEAL** WITH THAT STUFF.

OU DON'T HAVE TO BE RESPONSIBLE FOR ANYONE UNLESS YOU REALLY **WANT** TO BE.

YOU FIGHT YOUR WAY OUT FROM UNDER ALL THE POINTLESS FUCKING PARAPHERNALIA AND-- YOU'RE FREE. YOU'RE **YOURSELF**.

SO WHY AM I **ENJOYING** THIS? PLAYING **MOMMA**?

AND HOW AM I EVER GONNA LOOK *CUTLASS* IN THE *FACE* AGAIN?

WE'RE IN *IDZUMO*, IN SHIMANE PROVINCE. ABOUT FIVE MILES DOWN THE ROAD FROM THE *TAISHA* SHRINE.

BUT THAT'S *CRAZY*, STONE-FIST.

MIMI-SAMA SAID THE KEY WOULD TAKE US TO THE *SWORD-KING'S* HOUSE--IN THE REALM OF THE *KAMI*.

BUT WE'RE STILL IN OUR *OWN* WORLD-- THE NORMAL WORLD. IN THE MIDDLE OF *NOWHERE*.

AND NOW IT'S STOPPED WORKING ALTOGETHER.

THIS *ISN'T* THE MIDDLE OF NOWHERE, KAI. THIS IS NOWHERE'S STINKING, SHIT-CAKED *REAR END*.

THE ONLY *PHONE* HERE IS IN THE MAYOR'S HOUSE, AND THEY WOULDN'T EVEN LET ME IN.

THEY'VE NEVER SEEN ANYTHING *LIKE* ME HERE. BUT AT LEAST I GOT US A ROOM. AND TOMORROW WE CAN HITCH A RIDE AS FAR AS--

HEY, YOU! MAN-BITCH!

ME AND MY FRIENDS ARE THINKING OF *FUCKING* YOU.

OH YES?

BUT WE'RE NOT SURE IF YOU'D HAVE A *HOLE* IN THE RIGHT PLACE, 'CAUSE YOU LOOK LIKE A *HALF-AND-HALF!*

LIKE A *WHAT?*

YOU KNOW. HALF *MAN*, HALF WOMAN.

OH. I *GET* YOU NOW.

GUUUH!

YEAH, THAT'S WHAT I *AM.* YOU'VE GOT A SHARP *EYE.*

BUT MAYBE BEING *HALF* A MAN IS ENOUGH.

YOU'LL HAVE TO LET ME *KNOW.*

NN! NN! NNNNN!

ANYONE ELSE WANT A CUDDLE?

NO?

HEY, NICE TO MEET YOU BOYS. YOU REALLY KNOW HOW TO TURN A LADY'S *HEAD.*

DID YOU *HAVE* TO HURT HIM?

WHAT, THAT *BOTHERED* YOU? LOOK, A BIT OF VIOLENCE CAN BE LIKE--*OIL* ON THE WHEELS.

MAKE THINGS GO *SMOOTHER.*

THE KID LOOKS AWAY. OKAY, SO MAYBE I'LL HOLD BACK A LITTLE NEXT TIME. IF I KNOW HE'S WATCHING.

SHIT! I WONDER WHAT IT WOULD HAVE BEEN LIKE TO HAVE *HIS* CHILDHOOD.

TO KEEP AT LEAST A *LITTLE* BIT OF INNOCENCE.

TELL ME WHERE *KAIKOU HARA* IS.

OR I'M GOING TO HAVE TO *HURT* YOU.

SO *YOU'RE* THE SISTER HE WAS TALKING ABOUT? *TOSHI?*

THE ONE HE CROSSED HALF OF KYOTO FOR?

WELL, JUST *LOOKING* AT YOU HURTS *ME,* GIRL.

DOES IT?

LET ME EASE THE PAIN FOR YOU, THEN, YOU BLEACHED-OUT LITTLE TRAMP.

UFFF!

ARE YOU *READY* FOR THIS USO-TSUKI?

Of course, mistress.

GUUUUH!

SO CUT *DEEP.*

AND CUT *WIDE.*

AND YOU *KNOW* WHAT YOU'RE *LOOKING* FOR.

GUUUU--!

THIS *AIRHEAD* PROBABLY WON'T EVEN FEEL THE DIFFERENCE.

LOOK! THOSE ARE THE BODYGUARDS OF *MIMI OGUNO.* WE'RE MOVING IN *CIRCLES*--THE ASSASSIN FOLLOWING MY TRAIL AS I FOLLOW *HIS.*

BUT WE'VE *GOT* HIM NOW. WITH MIMI'S HELP WE CAN CLOSE THE NET.

UNLESS THIS GIRL-CHILD *WARNS* KAIKOU HARA THAT WE'RE COMING.

BUT SHE *WON'T.* IT'S GOING TO SLIP *COMPLETELY* OUT OF HER MIND.

I SUPPOSE--

--IT DEPENDS ON WHAT YOU'RE *USED* TO.

NO, IT REALLY *DOESN'T.* I HAD MY FILL OF PIGS AND POX-EATEN FACES AND PISSING IN A BUCKET A *LONG* TIME AGO.

I *LIKE* IT HERE. I LIKE HOW *PEACEFUL* IT IS.

WELL, LIE DOWN. IT'LL *PASS.*

I GREW UP IN A *SHIT-HOLE* LIKE THIS.

I LEFT BECAUSE I GOT TIRED OF BEING *GANG-RAPED* ON A FRIDAY NIGHT WHENEVER OLD MAN CHO WASN'T SHOWING A *MOVIE* AT THE TRACTOR GARAGE.

YOU WERE *RAPED?* THAT'S--GOD! STONE-FIST, THAT'S *TERRIBLE.*

I WAS JUST MAKING A *POINT,* KID. DON'T WORRY ABOUT IT.

COME ON OVER HERE. THERE'S SOMETHING *HAPPENING* DOWN IN THE STREET.

PILGRIMS. HEADING FOR THE *TAISHA* SHRINE.

WEIRD. *O-BON* WAS TWO WEEKS AGO. THERE'S NO *FESTIVAL* GOING ON RIGHT NOW.

THEN I THINK WE SHOULD *JOIN* THEM.

AND FIND OUT WHAT THEY'RE *CELEBRATING.*

WHY DID I EVEN **MENTION** THAT?

I **HATE** PEOPLE WHO WHINE ABOUT HOW HARD THEY HAD IT. LIKE IT EXPLAINS ANYTHING, OR **EXCUSES** ANYTHING.

BECAUSE IT **DOESN'T.**

NO MATTER WHAT **SHIT** POURS DOWN ON YOU, IT'S YOUR OWN **CHOICE** TO STAND UNDER IT OR MOVE OUT OF THE **WAY.**

WHAT **IS** THAT THING THEY'RE CARRYING?

IT'S A **PLOUGH.**

AND IT LOOKS LIKE THESE DUMB FUCKS DROVE IT INTO A ROCK.

SPIRITS, YOU SEE THE **FAVOR** THESE YOUR SUPPLICANTS HOPE AND PRAY FOR.

MAKE THIS IMPLEMENT **WHOLE,** I BEG YOU, THAT THEIR LIVELIHOODS SHOULD NOT BE PUT AT **RISK.**

P-PRAISE THEM! PRAISE THEIR HOLY NAMES!

GREAT-SOULED ONES, WE THANK YOU AND HONOR YOU IN OUR HEARTS.

TENKEI! *THANK* YOU, KIND SPIRITS!

BE *BLESSED* ABOVE ALL NAMES, AND ACCEPT OUR OFFERINGS!

STONE-FIST, LEND ME YOUR *KNIFE.*

WHAT?

THE KNIFE YOU WEAR ON YOUR *BELT.* LET ME BORROW IT FOR A MOMENT.

IF YOU'RE HERE, THEN WE'D LIKE TO *TALK--*

--ARATSU.

KRA-TISCHHH

ARE YOU ALL RIGHT?

I'M FINE. I'M JUST-- CUT.

IT'S NOTH--

...

KAI!

WAIT FOR *ME!* DON'T RUN OFF BY YOUR--

DON'T THINK HE EVEN HEARD ME. AND SUDDENLY THE SHRINE IS FULL OF PEOPLE YELLING AND WAVING THEIR **ARMS** AND ARGUING ABOUT WHETHER WHAT THEY'VE JUST SEEN WAS AN OMEN OR A **BLASPHEMY.**

BY THE TIME I GET **FREE**-- HE'S GONE.

BEEN A LONG WHILE, BUT IT'S ALL COMING BACK TO ME.

IN THE HEART OF THE COUNTRY, IF YOU KNOW THE **RUNNER** AND YOU DON'T KNOW THE MAN WHO'S **CHASING** HIM--

--YOU SUPPORT THE **HOME** TEAM. THAT'S GUARANTEED.

IN THE CITY, **EVERYONE'S** A STRANGER.

SO AT LEAST YOU'VE GOT A FIFTY-FIFTY **CHANCE.**

EXCUSE ME.

DID YOU SEE--?

THE KID LEARNS FAST, I'LL GIVE HIM THAT.

NO INSTINCT FOR THE JUGULAR, THOUGH. NO FOLLOW-THROUGH.

BUT THAT'S WHY MIMI-SAMA, IN HER INFINITE WISDOM--

--GAVE HIM A BIG-ASS GUARDIAN ANGEL.

HAHAHAHA! NO MATTER! NO MATTER!

I HAVE INK ENOUGH FOR A HUNDRED TOYS, A THOUSAND!

A HUNDRED THOUSAND MILL--

MAGIC INK?

NOT AFTER I'VE TOUCHED IT.

WHUDD

I HAD IT UNDER *CONTROL*, STONE-FIST.

WELL NOW IT'S *MORE* UNDER CONTROL.

YOUR RUNAWAY CLEANER WENT *THAT* WAY. UP THE STAIRS.

OKAY. I WANT TO TALK TO HIM.

WHY, EXACTLY?

JUST--THE WAY HE WAS *WATCHING* US AT THE SHRINE.

WILL YOU *WAIT* FOR ME?

OH, SURE. YOU GO AHEAD AND HAVE YOUR *CONVERSATION*.

THIS BUG-EYED *BASTARD* ISN'T GOING ANYWHERE.

THERE I GO AGAIN. WATCHING HIS *BACK* WHEN HE HASN'T ASKED ME TO.

FUCK YOUR MOTHER, I'LL BE WIPING HIS *NOSE* NEXT.

OKAY, WHOEVER YOU ARE.

I'M COMING IN.

SO DID THE **SWORD-KING** SEND YOU HERE? ARE YOU SPYING FOR HIM, IS THAT IT?

DID YOU SABOTAGE THE **KEY** TO BRING US TO YOU?

I-- MOP. BUCKET. SCRUB.

WALLS. FLOOR.

BUT THAT'S NOT ALL, IS IT? YOU WERE **WATCHING** ME.

WHY? DID SOMEONE **TELL** YOU I WAS COMING?

TELL? NOT--NO. NOT.

NOT **EVER** TELL. KNIVES.

UMM--OKAY. LET'S TRY A **DIFFERENT** QUESTION.

WHAT HAPPENED TONIGHT-- DOES IT HAPPEN **OFTEN**? SHARP THINGS GET **SHARPER**? SHINIER? MORE POINTY?

OKAY. COOL. AND...

...I THINK I'M GOING TO STOP *BOTHERING* YOU NOW.

THANKS FOR YOUR *HELP.*

HAH! HE FOUND A NEW *EMPLOYMENT,* DIDN'T HE? BUT KEPT HIS *COUNSEL.*

I *MISS* HIM. I MISS THEM *ALL.*

BUT I DON'T *BLAME* THEM!

WELL, GOOD.

WHAT COULD THEY *DO?*

UMM-- NOTHING, I GUESS.

MY HOUSE.

THANKS FOR YOUR TIME, OKAY? THIS IS--

BUY YOURSELF SOME *SAKE* OR SOMETHING.

HE DIDN'T KNOW *ANYTHING,* STONE-FIST. IT WAS ANOTHER *DEAD END.*

SO I WENT ON A **QUEST**. THAT'S WHAT IT COMES DOWN TO. AND WHAT I WAS LOOKING FOR WAS **MYSELF**.

HASHARITO, WHOEVER **SHE** IS.

I KNOW HOW **TIRED** THAT SOUNDS. I KNOW **EVERYBODY** SAYS IT.

MOSTLY WHEN THEY GET PAST **FORTY**. WHEN THE RHYTHMS OF THEIR **LIFE** START TO SEEM TOO FAMILIAR.

AND THEY WANT TO BELIEVE THERE'S **MORE** TO THEM THAN WHAT THEY DO FOR A LIVING.

BUT I DON'T MEAN THAT AT ALL.

I MEAN-- **LITERALLY.**

MY PAST IS A **HOLE**. NEATLY DUG, AND SQUARED OFF, LIKE A **GRAVE**.

AN EMPTY **SPACE** I THOUGHT I COULD FILL.

WHICH IS--SCARY, REALLY.

EVEN SCARIER THAN IT **SOUNDS.**

YOU'VE GOT TO BE ON YOUR **GUARD** THE WHOLE TIME.

YOU CAN'T TRUST **ANYBODY.**

I WAS LOOKING FOR YOU BECAUSE I WANTED TO BRING YOU *HOME*.

SHUT UP, ASSASSIN.

WELL, IT'S SORT OF *MOOT* NOW, ANYWAY.

--UNLESS YOU WANT TO KILL HIM IN FRONT OF A HUNDRED *WITNESSES*.

AND I COULD.

I COULD *EASILY*.

BUT SOMETHING IN THEIR *FACES* MAKES ME HESITATE.

SOMETHING THAT *CATCHES* ON THE EDGE OF THE HOLE IN MY MIND AND *HURTS*.

I CAN'T EXPLAIN. IT'S TOO *HARD*. MY MASTER TOOK MY PAST, AND HE'S THE ONLY ONE WHO CAN GIVE IT *BACK*.

NOTHING ELSE WILL DO. I CAN'T FILL THAT HOLE WITH *WORDS*, OR GOOD INTENTIONS.

GET THE KONDOBU OFF THE *STREET*, CUTLASS. INTO ONE OF THESE HOUSES.

WE'LL KILL IT *THERE*.

TOSHI, JUST LET ME *TELL* YOU ABOUT HOW ALL THIS HAPPENED. HOW WE--

PUT YOUR HAND OVER ITS *MOUTH* IF IT TALKS.

I DON'T WANT TO *LISTEN* TO IT.

HEY! YOU CAN'T COME IN HERE!

THIS IS A PRIVATE *HOUSE!* GET OUT BEFORE I--

AAA!

ONE MORE *WORD*. I'M ALREADY IN THE RIGHT MOOD.

JUST GIVE ME A *REASON* TO HURT YOU.

TAKE YOUR FAMILY *UPSTAIRS*. DON'T COME DOWN UNTIL WE'VE LEFT.

YOU'LL BE *SAFE* IF YOU STAY OUT OF MY WAY.

C-COME ALONG, RYUU. DO AS THE LADY *SAYS*.

BUT TAM-TAM--!

TAM-TAM WILL BE FINE. DON'T *ARGUE* WITH ME.

TURN IT *LOOSE*, CUTLASS.

AND GIVE IT YOUR *KNIFE*.

I DON'T *WANT* A KNIFE.

TAKE IT, KID.

IT'S THE BEST OFFER YOU'RE GOING TO *GET*.

WITH A KNIFE YOU'VE GOT A CHANCE TO *DEFEND* YOURSELF.

IF YOU'RE AS GOOD AS MY MASTER *SAYS* YOU ARE, IT WILL BE A FAIR FIGHT.

HOW CAN IT BE FAIR, WHEN KNIVES WON'T EVEN *CUT* YOU?

I WON'T *FIGHT* YOU, TOSHI.

LET ME KNOW WHEN YOU CHANGE YOUR *MIND*.

RRRRRRRRR

SEN! *BAD* DOG! BAD GIRL! LET ME *GO!*

KID--OH SHIT!

UUUH!

THIS IS FUCKING INSANE! IT'S JUST *TORTURE!*

IF SOMEONE'S OUT TO *GET* YOU, STONE, YOU HIT THEM FIRST.

WE'VE BOTH DONE *WORSE* THINGS IN OUR TIME.

IS THIS HOW ASSASSINS *WORK?* THEY STAND AROUND AND LET YOU KILL THEM AN *INCH* AT A TIME?

NONE OF THIS MAKES ANY *SENSE!*

GET OUT OF MY *WAY*, STONE-FIST.

SO YOU CAN TAKE OUT HIS *OTHER* EYE? FUCK YOU, GIRL.

WE'LL TAKE THIS TO *MIMI* AND SEE WHAT SHE SAYS.

NO.

CUT.

I'M **CUT.** I'M-- NO.

THAT CAN'T **HAPPEN.**

TOSHI, WAIT!

NO! NO! NO! **NO!**

DON'T--

STONE-FIST, DON'T LET HER GO. PLEASE! I'LL NEVER **FIND** HER AGAIN!

ALL RIGHT, KID. JUST--

I'LL SEE WHAT I CAN **DO.**

I DON'T EVEN KNOW WHAT I'M **RUNNING** FROM.

APART FROM--BEING **HURT.** BEING VULNERABLE.

IT'S WRONG. IT DOESN'T **HAPPEN** LIKE THAT, AND I WON'T LET IT.

NOBODY CAN **MAKE** ME.

CAN'T REMEMBER WHERE THE KONDOBU DOOR IS, BUT I STILL HAVE THE KEY KISHIMO-JIN GAVE ME.

I NEED TO GO TO MY *MASTER'S* HOUSE. THE HOUSE OF THE SWORD-KING. *NOTHING* CAN TOUCH ME THERE.

BUT MY THOUGHTS ARE WHIPPED TO *FROTH,* AND THE KEY STAYS *COLD* IN MY HAND.

WHAT'S WRONG WITH ME?

WHAT'S *WRONG* WITH ME?

TOSHI.

HOLD YOUR *HORSES,* GIRL.

KEEP *AWAY* FROM ME, CUTLASS!

WHY DIDN'T YOU HELP ME WHEN I *NEEDED* YOU?

BECAUSE STONE-FIST IS *RIGHT.* SOMETHING HERE STINKS.

YOU SHOULD COME ON BACK AND *TALK* TO THE BOY.

WHAT HAVE YOU GOT TO *LOSE?*

EVERYTHING! I CAN'T--

I WON'T KNOW IF HE'S *LYING* TO ME! THE ONLY WAY I CAN KNOW IS IF I GET MY *MEMORIES* BACK.

WE'RE NOT SAYING YOU SHOULD *TRUST* HIM. JUST HEAR HIM OUT.

BUT-- IT WASN'T **THEM** THAT I WAS ANGRY WITH. IT WAS **ME!**

Then I suppose you'd best learn to keep your anger on a tighter **leash.**

I JUST-- I WANTED MY **MEMORIES** BACK. I WANTED TO BE **MYSELF** AGAIN.

I WANTED IT SO **MUCH.**

BUT WHENEVER I THINK ABOUT THE PAST NOW--**THIS** WILL BE IN IT.

That's true.

UNLESS...

USO-TSUKI, I NEED A **FAVOR.**

Anything, mistress. What is it?

I'VE CHANGED MY **MIND.**

TAKE MY MEMORIES OF THIS PLACE **AWAY.** THE BOY. CUTLASS AND STONE-FIST. EVERYTHING.

I DON'T WANT TO KNOW WHAT I **DID** TONIGHT.

But-- your memories ere meant to be ur *reward*. That's what you were *fighting* for.

BECAUSE I FELT THEIR *ABSENCE.* LIKE A HOLE INSIDE ME.

BUT PERHAPS IF I FORGET *ENOUGH*--

--I WON'T EVEN KNOW ANY-MORE WHAT I'M *MISSING.* AND THEN I'LL BE HAPPY.

THE BLADES DIDN'T HURT GOING IN. I WASN'T REALLY *EXPECTING* THEM TO.

BUT THE *PAST*--

THE PAST AS IT PILLED OUT OF E FELT LIKE OLD *AIR* ACROSS N ACHING TOOTH.

ALMOST A *SOUND,* AT THE LIMIT OF HEARING. MY OWN VOICE SCREAMING, HIGH ENOUGH TO SCARE THE--

--DOGS. THE *DOGS.*

WHERE'S--?

WHERE DID SHE--?

Are you *well*, mistress?

QUITE WELL, USO-TSUKI. BUT WHERE *ARE* WE?

DID YOU-- *TAKE* SOMETHING FROM ME? A MEMORY?

Yes, because you *asked* me to. We are in Idzumi.

But our business here is done, and now we are going *home*.

OUR *BUSINESS?* WAS IT RELATED IN SOME WAY TO THESE *CORPSES?*

No. Not in the slightest.

These were *strangers* over whose remains you just said a brief *prayer*.

THEN LET'S GO HOME.

MY DEAR AND FAITHFUL FRIEND.

I WAS *WRONG* ABOUT THE PAST. THAT'S *OBVIOUS.*

WRONG TO THINK I *NEEDED* IT.

OR AT LEAST--THERE MUST BE A **HIGH** ROAD AND A **LOW** ROAD TO HAPPINESS.

HOW **STRANGE** NOT TO HAVE SEEN THAT BEFORE.

THAT FORGETFULNESS **ARMORS** YOU AGAINST ALMOST EVERY PAIN THERE IS.

AND MAKES EVERY MORNING LIKE ANOTHER **BIRTH.**

SO WE RAN **TOGETHER** THROUGH THE NIGHT.

A BOY, A MAN, A DEMON, AND THE GHOST OF A **DOG**.

AND WHY?

BECAUSE SHE TOLD US TO.

BECAUSE SHE TOLD US TO, AND I WASN'T **STRONG** ENOUGH YET TO PULL OUT OF HER **ORBIT**.

NIDORU--

--I HAVE TO GO FIND MY **SISTER**.

NO, KAIKOU HARA. YOU HAVE TO DO WHAT YOU'RE **TOLD**.

OR ELSE YOU COULD **DIE**.

DEATH IS **ALWAYS** AN OPTION.

The Last Word

THEY'RE NOT HERE. IT'S BEEN MORE THAN AN *HOUR* NOW.

IF *STONE-FIST* DIDN'T FIND HER--

SIT DOWN. AND BE *SILENT.*

GLASS, YOU CARRY THE *SEEDS* OF SHARPNESS.

MY MASTER LOVES YOU, AND YOU SWORE *FEALTY* TO HIM ONCE.

ONEGAI SHIMASU.

WHAT ARE YOU DOING?

MAKING *BARRICADES.* MY MASTER'S NAME HAS BEEN SPOKEN.

THOSE WHO WISH HIM *HARM* WILL COME.

BUT MY MASTER *RINJIN* WILL COME TOO, AS SOON AS HE KNOWS.

IT FALLS ON ME TO KEEP US ALL *ALIVE* UNTIL HE ARRIVES.

AND SO I BUILD *WALLS.* HOPING THAT EACH ONE WILL *DELAY* OUR ENEMIES AT LEAST A LITTLE.

MASTER, WILL IT PLEASE YOU TO *SIT?*

PLEASE, NIDORU.

I HAVE TO *FIND* HER. LET ME GO.

YOU'RE VERY *BEAUTIFUL.*

I THINK I SEWED A *GARMENT* WITH YOU ONCE. OR WAS THAT YOUR MOTHER?

MASTER, IT WAS I. YOU HONOR ME.

IF YOU LEAVE THIS ROOM, IT'S UNLIKELY YOU'LL *SURVIVE* FOR MORE THAN A MOMENT OR TWO.

I DON'T SEE ANY *ENEMIES.*

WHEN YOU SEE THEM, IT WILL BE TOO *LATE.* TRUST ME. WE'LL FIND YOUR SISTER *LATER.*

FINE.

GOOD, THEN. A WALL OF STEEL, A WALL OF GLASS.

AND NOW WE BUILD A WALL OF *TRUTH.*

WHAT DOES *THAT* MEAN?

EACH ONE *ASKS,* AND EACH ONE ANSWERS. THE QUESTION MATTERS NOT, SO LONG AS THE ANSWER IS *TRUE.*

TRUTH WILL BE OUR *FORTRESS.* MASTER, FORGIVE MY PRESUMPTION--

--BUT WHAT IS THE FIRST THING YOU *REMEMBER?*

THE FIRST THING--?

UP UNTIL THAT DAY--YOU WERE A *KING.*

WAS I? I DON'T *REMEMBER.*

THAT'S *WEIRD.* IT'S-- IT'S KIND OF LIKE--

RESCHHHHHH

HE'S HERE! THE SWORD-KING IS HERE!

THE *FORMER* SWORD-KING.

WHAT *WONDROUS* GOOD FORTUNE. TONIGHT WE EAT *KAMI.*

YOUR TURN, KAIKOU HARA.

MY LORD, IF IT PLEASE YOU-- ASK THE BOY A *QUESTION*.

HE SEEMS-- AFRAID. OF *MANY* THINGS.

I SHOULD LIKE TO KNOW WHAT THING *FRIGHTENS* HIM MORE THAN ANY OTHER.

GIVE US THE *TRUTH*.

WHAT? I DON'T EVEN--*LOTS* OF THINGS SCARE ME.

THEN SPEAK *QUICKLY*. SPEAK WHAT RISES IN YOUR *MIND* RIGHT NOW.

...

THE *SPEAR-THROWER*.

"I WAS TEN YEARS OLD. AND THE SPEAR-THROWER WAS THE MEDIA'S NICKNAME FOR NAGASAKI'S FIRST EVER *SERIAL KILLER.*

"WHO WAS ALREADY UP TO HIS *FOURTH* VICTIM.

"HE HAD TO BE ENORMOUSLY *STRONG,* THEY SAID. BECAUSE HIS VICTIMS WERE ALL STRONG, CAPABLE MEN.

"AND BECAUSE THE CAUSE OF DEATH WAS A SINGLE *PUNCTURE* WOUND. SOMETHING HAD BEEN DRIVEN STRAIGHT *THROUGH* THEIR CHEST OR ABDOMEN WITH HORRENDOUS FORCE."

--FOUND FLAKES OF *RUST* IN THE CHEST CAVITY OF THE KILLER'S FOURTH VICTIM, BANKER *KINICHI ENDO--*

--LEADING POLICE TO SPECULATE THAT THE KILLER'S WEAPON OF CHOICE IS A SHARPENED IRON *ROD* THREE INCHES IN DIAMETER.

"I IMAGINED A *GIANT* HEFTING AN IRON SPEAR AS HEAVY AS A GROWN *MAN.*

"AND I WAS AFRAID TO *SLEEP* IN CASE I SAW HIM IN MY DREAMS.

"WITH *PREDICTABLE* RESULTS."

WHAT'S HAPPENED TO MY BEST STUDENT? THIS ISN'T *LIKE* YOU, KAI.

I--I'M SORRY, HINO-SAMA. I WAS *TIRED.*

"I HAD A BIG *CRUSH* ON MISS HINO. MOST OF THE BOYS IN THE CLASS DID.

"SHE WAS SO *BEAUTIFUL*, AND SO SOFT-SPOKEN. SO PATIENT WITH US.

"BUT ONCE, WHEN SHE WAS WRITING ON THE *BOARD*, I SAW--I THOUGHT I SAW--

"IT MADE NO SENSE. WHO WOULD *HURT* HINO-SAMA IN THAT WAY?"

SO WHAT'S KEEPING YOU *AWAKE* AT NIGHTS, KAI?

N-NOTHING, HINO-SAMA. I'M JUST--

I THINK MY *MIND* IS TOO ACTIVE.

WELL, THAT GOES WITH THE *TERRITORY* FOR A LITTLE GENIUS LIKE YOU.

YOU CAN STILL BE MY BEST STUDENT IF YOU CARRY MY *BAG* FOR ME.

"HINO-SAMA WAS VERY FRAIL BECAUSE SHE HAD *MULTIPLE SCLEROSIS.* WE ALL KNEW, BECAUSE THE PRINCIPAL HAD TOLD US IN ASSEMBLY.

"SHE TOOK ME TO THE *EUROPEAN* QUARTER-- A VERY UP-MARKET ADDRESS FOR A *SHOGAKKO* TEACHER."

OH! HINO-SAMA, IS THIS *YOUR* HOUSE?

IT WAS MY *FATHER'S.* I'M LIVING HERE UNTIL I CAN *SELL* IT.

IN THE 1800s, IT BELONGED TO THE JEWISH *MERCHANT* ISAAC VALDEZ. WOULD YOU LIKE A GUIDED *TOUR?*

AND BEHIND THE *KITCHEN* THERE ARE TWO STONE PANTRIES-- ONE FOR DAIRY FOODS AND ONE FOR *MEAT.*

BUT DOWN IN THE BASEMENT-- THERE IS THE *REAL* TREASURE.

COME AND *SEE.*

THAT'S A *MEZUZAH.* A JEWISH GOOD LUCK CHARM. THERE'S ONE ON EVERY *DOOR.*

YOU'VE GOT YOUR OWN *SWIMMING POOL?*

IT'S A *MIKVAH.* A RITUAL BATH.

BUT THE WATER IS SO *DARK.*

MENTHOL OIL. IT'S ALSO VERY, VERY COLD.

YOU HAVE A *HOT* BATH AND THEN YOU COME DOWN HERE AND JUMP STRAIGHT IN.

IT'S FOR MY *SPECIAL* FRIENDS, AND FOR ME. IT'S GOOD FOR THE *PAINS* IN MY JOINTS.

"THE BASEMENT WAS DARK. MY FEARS *ROSE* IN MY THROAT.

"IT WAS--I NEVER FAINTED IN MY *LIFE,* BUT SUDDENLY THE TILED FLOOR SLOPED AND BUCKED LIKE A SHIP'S *DECK."*

KAI--!

MMNUH-- DON'T--FEEL...

YOU ALMOST *FELL.* INTO THE POOL. LISTEN TO ME, KAI. I'LL TELL YOU SOMETHING ABOUT *FEAR.*

SOMETHING EVEN MY *FATHER*--THE BIGGEST, STRONGEST MAN I EVER MET-- NEVER *LEARNED.*

FEAR IS LIKE A LITTLE *GOBLIN* THAT SITS IN FRONT OF A LANTERN.

FROM A *DISTANCE* YOU ONLY SEE THE SHADOW HE CASTS, AND THE SHADOW IS ENORMOUS.

BUT ONCE YOU GET UP *CLOSE,* YOU REALIZE HOW TINY HE IS.

AND ONCE YOU *KNOW* THAT-- HE'LL NEVER HAVE ANY *POWER* OVER YOU, EVER AGAIN.

"AFTER THAT I WAS MORE *MOONSTRUCK* THAN EVER.

"THE SPEAR-THROWER WAS STILL *OUT* THERE, DOING HIS THING. BUT MY DREAMS WERE TOO *FULL* NOW, TO ALLOW HIM ANY ROOM.

"I DIDN'T *CRY* WHEN SHE DIED. I WAS IN *KOUTOGAKKOU*--BIG SCHOOL--BY THEN, SO CRYING WASN'T AN *OPTION.*

"BUT I SAT IN MY *ROOM* FOR WEEKS. NOT EVEN *TOSHI* COULD SNAP ME OUT OF IT.

"THREE OR FOUR MONTHS LATER, MUM AND DAD WERE THINKING OF *MOVING* TO A BIGGER PLACE.

"THE ESTATE AGENT WANTED TO SHOW US A PROPERTY IN THE EUROPEAN QUARTER THAT HAD COME UP FOR *SALE.*

"IT WAS *HERS,* OF COURSE."

PLENTY OF *ROOM,* YES?

AND IT'S VERY LIGHT AND *AIRY,* WHICH OLD HOUSES OFTEN AREN'T.

WHAT'S DOWN *HERE?*

WELL, APPARENTLY, IT WAS SOME KIND OF *HOT TUB* OR SPA.

BUT THE *SEAL* CRACKED AND THEY HAD TO DRAIN IT. NO DAMAGE TO THE *FOUNDATIONS,* AND IT COULD EASILY BE REPAIRED.

OF COURSE YOU'D HAVE TO REMOVE *THAT* MONSTROSITY, TOO.

NOBODY'S QUITE SURE WHAT IT'S *THERE* FOR.

"THE SPEAR-THROWER HADN'T *NEEDED* TO BE ALL THAT STRONG AFTER ALL. GRAVITY AND *MOMENTUM* HAD DONE MOST OF THE HARD WORK FOR HER.

"I JUST WISH I COULD HAVE ASKED HER *WHY.*

"AND MAYBE-- HOW SHE GOT THE BODIES *OUT* OF THE POOL AFTERWARDS."

WHAT?

TOSHI AND ME. WHY ARE WE DIFFERENT? FROM EVERYONE ELSE, AND FROM EACH OTHER?

TELL ME THAT, IF YOU KNOW.

I PRAY YOU--ASK ME SOME OTHER QUESTION.

THAT MATTER I DO NOT CARE TO SPEAK OF.

HEY, YOU PUT ME THROUGH THE WRINGER, AND NOW YOU'RE CRYING OFF?

THAT STINKS, NIDORU.

NONETHELESS. YOU'LL HAVE TO CHOOSE ANOTHER--

ANSWER HIM.

M-MY LORD?

ANSWER HIS QUESTION.

IT SEEMS FAIR.

I--I OBEY.

AS ALWAYS.

"LONG AGO, THERE WAS A LADY--*NIJIRA HARA*, YOUR ANCESTOR--WHOSE HUSBAND *LEFT* HER TO FIGHT IN A DISTANT WAR.

"SUCH THINGS WERE *COMMON* THEN, AS NOW.

"SHE *PRAYED* DAY AND NIGHT FOR HIS SAFE RETURN.

"THUS DID *KNIVES* HAVE KNOWLEDGE OF HER.

"HE CAME TO HER AND PROPOSED A *BARGAIN.*

"AND *CUT* HERSELF, BOTH TO SHOW FORTITUDE AND TO OFFER UP HER *PAIN* TO THE KAMI.

"AND WHAT KNIVES KNOW, MY *MASTER* KNOWS. FOR HE IS THE *KING* OF KNIVES.

"FOR ONE *BOON* FROM HER, HE WOULD GRANT HER HUSBAND FREE PASSAGE. SWORDS AND ARROWS, POINT AND EDGE, WOULD NOT *HARM* HIM, THEN OR EVER.

"AND IN RETURN SHE GAVE HIM HER *BODY.*

"*BETRAYING* HER HUSBAND IN ORDER TO ENSURE HIS *SAFE* RETURN."

YOU--YOU HAD **SEX?** YOU AND LADY NIJIRA HARA?

THEN THAT'S WHY TOSHI CAN'T BE **CUT?**

YOU ASK A **QUESTION,** AND THEN WILL NOT HEAR THE ANSWER.

THERE IS NO **STOPPING** THIS NOW, KAIKOU HARA. THE **TRUTH** MUST BE TOLD.

"MY LORD **KEPT** HIS WORD. BUT HEARING THAT NIJIRA WAS WITH CHILD, HE SUMMONED ME TO HIM.

"'I DID NOT DESIRE AN **HEIR,**' HE SAID. 'GO TO THE LADY, AND CUT AWAY THE **DIVINE** PART OF THE CHILD SO THAT IT IS BORN HUMAN.'

"AND THIS I **DID,** WHILE THE LADY SLEPT.

"**EXCISING** MY MASTER'S ESSENCE FROM THE CHILD'S FRAME--LEAVING BEHIND NOTHING BUT BARE **HUMANITY.**

"WOULD THAT I COULD HAVE CUT NIJIRA HARA FROM MY MASTER'S **MIND** SO EASILY.

"BUT I COULD NOT. AS THE DAYS PASSED, HIS THOUGHTS TURNED TO HER MORE AND MORE."

"AT LAST HE CAME TO HER *AGAIN,* IN HIS MAJESTY."

"AND SHE--*SLUT* THAT SHE WAS--RECEIVED HIM WITH JOY."

"FORGETTING HER *MARRIAGE* VOWS, AND GIVING FREELY WHAT ERST SHE HAD *BARGAINED* FOR."

"IT WAS NOT *RIGHT.* FOR HER IT WAS UNLAWFUL. FOR HIM--*DEMEANING.*"

"MY HEART *SICKENED* AS I WATCHED. AND I KNEW MY *DUTY.*"

"THIS TIME I DID NOT *WAIT* TO BE TOLD."

"I WENT TO HER IN THE NIGHT WHERE SHE LAY, HER *BELLY* SWELLING WITH MY MASTER'S *SEED.*"

"BUT MY HAND *SHOOK,* AND I CUT TOO DEEP. TOOK AWAY SOME OF THE CHILD'S *HUMANITY* AS WELL AS ITS DIVINE PART."

"WHAT WAS LEFT WAS NEITHER GOD NOR MAN. IT WAS THE FIRST *KONDOBU.* THE ABYSS-SOUL WHOSE TOUCH ALL THINGS FEAR."

"MY SIN--MY SIN WAS *GREAT.*"

"BUT *STILL* IT DID NOT END. STILL MY MASTER AND THE BITCH *RUTTED* LIKE ANIMALS.

"UNTIL--FOR THE THIRD AND *FINAL* TIME--HER WOMB QUICKENED.

"BLADES ARE MY *NATURE.* I NEVER MISS. I NEVER FALTER.

"THE TIME BEFORE, I HAD BEEN--*DISTRACTED.* NOW I WAS CALM, AND *CLEAR* IN MY THOUGHTS.

"BUT THE LADY *WOKE,* AND FOUGHT ME.

"AND THOUGH I CUT TRUE, SHE WAS *MOVING.* SHE TRIED TO TWIST *AWAY* FROM THE STROKE.

"I CUT *HER* INSTEAD OF THE CHILD. CUT HER TOO DEEPLY TO *MEND.*

"SHE GAVE *BIRTH* AS SHE DIED, AND THE CHILD WAS TRULY MY MASTER'S *HEIR.*

"I HAD *FAILED.*

"SO HAS IT BEEN IN YOUR *LINE* IN EVERY *GENERATION* SINCE. ONE HUMAN CHILD, ONE KONDOBU AND ONE KAMI--ALWAYS IN THAT *ORDER.*

"AND SINCE YOUR *FATHER* WAS THE HUMAN SEED, YOUR OWN NATURE--AND YOUR *SISTER'S*-- WERE EASY THINGS TO PREDICT."

M-MY GOD!

THE WALL OF WORDS HELD.

YOU SPOKE *TRULY* ABOUT YOUR FEARS.

AND SO DID *YOU*, ABOUT YOUR SIN.

YES. THOUGH I WISH WITH ALL MY *HEART* THAT I COULD HAVE LIED.

I SEE YOUR PAIN IN YOUR FACE, AND IT *SHAMES* ME. I CAN ONLY OFFER--

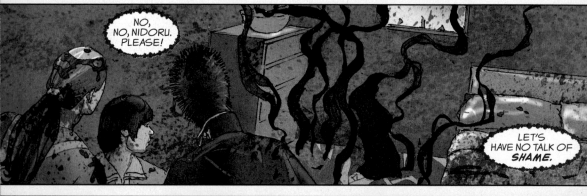

NO, NO, NIDORU. PLEASE!

LET'S HAVE NO TALK OF *SHAME*.

THIS IS A *JOYOUS* OCCASION. MINSTRELS SHOULD SING, AND MUSICIANS *PLAY* FOR US.

FIREWORKS SHOULD PAINT THE SKIES.

SWORD-KING, I AM *KUMORI-RINJIN*, THE EARL OF SHADOWS.

YOU ARE UNDER *MY* PROTECTION NOW. AS ARE ALL THIS COMPANY.

RRRRRRRRRRRRR

YOU'VE DONE *WELL*, KAIKOU HARA. NIDORU SAID YOU WOULD.

I OFFER YOU A *COMMISSION* IN MY ARMY. BE MY GENERAL, AND WREST THE SWORD-KING'S *SCEPTRE* FROM ARATSU'S UNWORTHY HAND.

ONLY IF I CAN FREE MY *SISTER*, TOO.

AND ON ONE OTHER CONDITION.

PLEASE TO *NAME* IT.

TAKE THIS *FILTH* OUT OF MY SIGHT.

PUT IT SOMEWHERE WITHOUT *AIR* OR SUNLIGHT, AND NEVER LET IT *OUT*.

AH, BUT NIDORU IS NIDORU. I KNOW NOT HOW SUCH A THING MIGHT BE *DONE*.

I WILL SUBMIT TO KAIKOU HARA'S JUDGMENT. MY MASTER HAS HEARD ME *CONFESS* MY SHAME.

UNTIL IT'S *EXPIATED*, I WILL NOT STAND BEFORE HIM AGAIN.

FAREWELL, MASTER. I HOPE YOU WILL AT LAST *FORGIVE* ME.

PERHAPS MY SERVICE TO YOU HERE COUNTS SOMEWHAT AGAINST MY *TRESPASS*.

GOODBYE. I'VE ENJOYED *MEETING* YOU.

THEN ALL'S WELL. YOU CAN ENTER MY SERVICE *IMMEDIATELY*, BOY.

I SUPPOSE I CAN. BUT I SHOULD BE *TOLD* WHAT IT IS I'M FACING.

OF COURSE. WHAT WOULD YOU LIKE TO *KNOW*?

ARATSU'S SWORD.

HOW DOES IT *WORK*?

THE QUESTION I WOULD HAVE YOU **ASK** YOURSELVES, MY LORDS, MY BROTHERS, IS A VERY **SIMPLE** ONE.

AND YET IT IS **PROFOUND.**

WHAT HAVE WE **BECOME?**

ARATSU WAS A SERVING MAN. A **MADE** THING. HE OWED HIS LIFE AND BEING TO THE **SWORD-KING,** ASIROSAMIRO.

YET HOW DID ARATSU **REPAY** THAT DEBT?

HE **REBELLED.** TOOK FROM HIS RIGHTFUL **MASTER** ALL THAT WAS HIS.

ONLY **TWO** STAYED LOYAL--THE STEWARD **YAMADA** AND THE WARRIOR, GREAT **NIDORU.**

WHO FOUND HER LORD AT LAST AND BROUGHT HIM **HOME.**

TOOK THRONE, SUBJECTS, NAME AND HONORS. EVERYTHING BUT **BREATH.**

WHAT **SAY** YOU, BROTHERS? IF YOU WOULD **ADDRESS** THIS INJUSTICE, STAND.

STAND AND BE **COUNTED.**

LET THE EARTH AND THE HEAVENS SEE THAT *HONOR* IS NOT DEAD!

"There are only two forces in the world, the sword and the soul. Over a long enough distance, the soul — so far — has always won..." — *Napoleon Bonaparte*

THE SWORD IN THE SOUL

YOU SEEM *THOUGHTFUL*, MASTER HARA.

I JUST-- COULDN'T BELIEVE HOW *MANY* OF THEM THERE WERE.

AND THEY ALL *WENT* WITH IT. THEY ALL SIGNED UP.

YES. THAT *RABBLE* WILL NOT WIN A WAR, HOWEVER. I'VE SENT LETTERS TO THE *DEATH GODS* AND THE *FIRE-KEEPERS*.

THEIR SUPPORT IS *CRUCIAL* IF WE'RE TO DEFEAT ARATSU.

WELL, WHILE YOU'RE WAITING FOR A *REPLY*, I'M GOING BACK TO TOKYO.

I ADVISE *AGAINST* IT. YOU'RE SAFER HERE.

I DON'T CARE. IF I *DIE* IN THIS FIGHT, I WANT MY MUM AND DAD TO KNOW WHAT *HAPPENED* TO ME.

IF YOU ARE SO *RESOLVED*-- SABURO.

YES, LORD RINJIN.

ESCORT KAIKOU HARA TO THE *GREY WORLD*. GO VIA RENJI'S FOLD, AND TAKE CARE THAT YOU'RE NOT *FOLLOWED*.

TAKE NO LONGER THAN THREE HOURS, MASTER HARA. I'LL EXPECT YOU HERE AT THE START OF THE FOURTH WATCH.

FOR OUR COUNCIL OF *WAR*.

NO, CARRION THING, IT IS **NOT**! LIKE **EVERYTHING** ABOUT YOU, IT IS MINE.

AND YOU LIVE OR DIE AT MY **WHIM**. DO YOU UNDERSTAND?

YES, LORD. I UNDERSTAND, AND PRAY YOUR **PARDON**.

HOW MAY I **SERVE** YOU, LORD?

BETTER. THE MAN AT THE TAISHA SHRINE, WH STOOD **AGAINS** YOU AND BROKE YOUR **BLADE**.

WAS **THIS** HIS FACE?

YES. HE LOOKS **OLDER** NOW, BUT--

--THAT'S THE MAN I **SAW**.

IT IS HE, THEN. **ASIROSAMIRO**, RETURNED.

SHALL I **FIND** HIM AGAIN AND KILL HIM?

I THINK **NOT**.

HE MET **AIDONO'S** BLADE, JUST AS YOU DID. AND FRO THAT **KISS** THER IS NO TURNING BACK.

NO, OUR **CHIEF** CONCERN LIES ELSEWHERE.

AND YOU **KNOW** ITS NAME.

SO YOU SERVE THE LORD OF CLOSED DOORS?

THE *SHADOW-DRAGON*, THOUGH, HE'S A DEEP ONE, ISN'T HE?

KEEPS THAT HUMAN *BOY* AT HIS SIDE, THAT NEVER HAS A WORD TO SAY FOR ITSELF. SOME KIND OF *PET*, I'M THINKING.

HARSH, BUT FAIR, I'D SAY. HE *FLOGGED* ME ONCE FOR STARING AT HIS DAUGHTER. FORTY STROKES.

IS HE NOT A *STERN* MASTER?

BUT HE BADE THE TORTURER STOP THE WOUNDS WITH *MERCURY*, AFTER.

THAT'S NO HUMAN.

THAT'S A *KONDOBU*.

AAAA!

PLAGUE TAKE IT. GIVE A MAN FAIR **WARNING** BEFORE YOU BANDY WORDS LIKE THAT.

AND THAT'S WHY RINJIN WAITS ON HIS **RETURN** BEFORE HE HAS HIS COUNCIL OF WAR.

YOU'LL SEE THE **FLAG** GO UP OVER THAT TENT TO SIGNIFY HE'S NOT TO BE DISTURBED. BUT IT'LL NOT FLY BEFORE **KAIKOU HARA** IS SAFELY BACK IN CAMP.

STRANGE **COMPANY** WE'RE KEEPING.

WOULD YOU RATHER FIGHT **AGAINST** A KONDOBU, OR ALONGSIDE ONE?

HAH! A SOUND **POINT,** TO BE SURE.

HRRRRR!

WHAT'S THE **MATTER,** KAMA-ITACHI?

I KNOW NOT, BUDO. IT'S LIKE SOMEONE JUST WALKED OVER MY **GRAVE.**

OKAY, YOU **GOT** IT.

BUT IS THAT WHAT YOU **REALLY** CAME HERE FOR, COUNTRY BOY?

UMM-- YES. WHY ELSE?

I THOUGHT MAYBE YOU CAME TO PAY YOUR **DEBTS.**

"SEX SLAVE FOR A **DAY.**" REMEMBER?

I--THAT WAS--I THOUGHT YOU WERE JUST-- YOU KNOW, JOKING.

ABOUT **SEX?** UH-UH.

LORETTA, I DON'T **HAVE** A DAY.

THEN YOU'D BETTER GET **STARTED--**

--HADN'T YOU?

112

So we prepare for *war*, mistress.

YES, *USO-TSUKI*. WE DO.

AND WARRIORS CAN'T *AFFORD* DOUBTS OR SCRUPLES.

You want me to *cut* you again. Cut away the few memories you have left. Mistress, do not *ask* it of me.

I DON'T ASK IT. I *REQUIRE* IT.

PARTICULARLY-- REMOVE ANYTHING THAT CONCERNS THE *BOY* OR THE DOG I LOST.

This isn't about strength. You think to remove the *hurt* by removing your own *knowledge* of it.

But those memories are rooted in your *soul*.

MY SOUL IS A *BLADE*, USO-TSUKI.

A BLADE MUST *NARROW* TO ITS POINT. TO ITS EDGE.

MAKE ME--

--AS *SHARP* AS YOU CAN.

113

SO-- --HOW WAS IT FOR YOU?

IT WAS INCREDIBLE.

JUST-- INCREDIBLE?

VERY INCREDIBLE.

GOOD. THERE'S MORE WHERE THAT CAME FROM, YOU KNOW.

WHEN I COME BACK--

I MEANT RIGHT NOW.

YOUR SISTER HAS TURNED INTO THIS NINJA-GHOST THING WITH MAGIC SCISSORS.

SHE WANTS TO KILL YOU. AND IF YOU DON'T BAIL OUT OF THIS, THAT'S WHAT SHE'LL END UP DOING.

WHAT? DID I THINK THE UNTHINKABLE?

SHE'S ALREADY GONE, KAI. YOU'VE LOST HER. IF YOU SAW HER, YOU'D KNOW WHAT I MEAN.

I DID SEE HER.

SHE TOOK OUT MY EYE.

IS THAT A WEIRD *METAPHOR*, OR--NO, YOU REALLY *MEAN* IT, DON'T YOU?

SHIT, KAI, WHAT ARE YOU TRYING TO DO? OFFER HER A *TWO-FOR-ONE* DEAL?

I JUST--I HAVE TO FIND HER. I'M REALLY *CLOSE* NOW. I'VE GOT HELP.

PSYCHIATRIC HELP, YOU MEAN? SHE'S A *KILLER*, KAI. YOU'RE--A NICE GUY WITH A *LITTLE-BOY-LOST* VIBE I FIND KIND OF SEXY.

SHE WILL FUCKING *EAT* YOU ALIVE.

MAYBE SHE *WILL.* BUT I CAN'T JUST GIVE UP ON HER, LORETTA.

YES, YOU *CAN.* RIGHT NOW, YOU *CAN.*

BEFORE IT GETS EVEN SICKER AND BLOODIER AND *STUPIDER* THAN IT ALREADY IS.

YOU CAN SAY *GOODBYE.*

GOODBYE.

WHEN WILL THIS COUNCIL BEGIN?

RINJIN WAITS FOR HIS LITTLE *HUMAN.* AND DRAGS OUR DIGNITY THROUGH THE DUST.

BE SURE TO *TELL* HIM SO, WHEN HE RETURNS. I'M NEXT IN *LINE* FOR YOUR COMMISSION.

MY LORD.

KAIKOU HARA HAS RETURNED.

YOU'RE *LATE,* MASTER HARA. WENT YOUR BUSINESS WELL?

I'D RATHER NOT *TALK* ABOUT IT.

EXCELLENT. I AGREE MOST *READILY.*

I HAVE A *GIFT* FOR YOU, AND IT MUST BE OPENED NOW.

BEFORE WE GO INTO *COUNCIL.*

THEIR ANSWER WAS *NO.*

LORDS, LOOK NOT SO *AMAZED.*

IF WE GO NOW TO ARATSU'S *FORTRESS,* AND PEN HIM IN BEFORE HE CAN TAKE THE FIELD...

...WHY, THEN, HIS *NUMBERS* WILL MAKE NO--

BUT--WE *DEPENDED* ON--

ONLY CONSIDER. IF WE ACT *QUICKLY,* THE ADVANTAGE CAN STILL BE OURS.

THE *SIEGE ENGINES* PROMISED TO US ARE OUR GREATEST ASSET.

...

≶SNF≷
SNF

KILL HER, WARRIORS. KILL THIS *CHILD* YOU SEE BEFORE YOU.

ALL ATTACKS, ALL *WEAPONS*, ARE PERMISSIBLE. AND LORD ARATSU'S BOUNTY GOES TO *ALL* OF YOU IF ANY *ONE* SUCCEEDS.

YOU MUST *DIE*, LITTLE ONE, SO THAT WE MAY *PROSPER*.

BUT GIVE US YOUR *PARDON*, AND YOU'LL HAVE SUCH MERCY AS WE CAN GRANT.

A *QUICK* DEATH, AND NO DISHONOR.

MY PARDON? YOU *HAVE* IT, SOLDIER.

BUT YOUR MERCY WON'T BE *REQUIRED*.

AND **THEN** WHAT?

GO ON, **DODOMEKI.** TELL ME WHAT YOU HEARD.

MY LORD, THE SHADOW-DRAGON TOLD HIS GENERALS THAT THE **DEATH-GODS** HAD REFUSED TO JOIN WITH HIM.

SO HIS ONLY REAL STRENGTH NOW LIES IN THE **SIEGE ENGINES.** HE HOPES TO PEN YOU UP, HERE IN YOUR **FORTRESS,** BEFORE YOU CAN TAKE THE FIELD.

AND THE **KONDOBU** WAS THERE, YOU SAY?

YES, MY LORD. IN BLACK **ARMOR** THAT WAS ALL OVER POINTS AND JAGS.

BUT AT THAT POINT I WAS **DISCOVERED** AND HAD TO FLEE.

YOU DID **WELL,** DODOMEKI. LEAVE US NOW.

I'LL ALLOW YOU TO SLEEP FOR SEVEN YEARS BEFORE I CALL ON YOU AGAIN.

MY LORD IS MOST **GRACIOUS.**

WHAT THINK YOU, *MUMBU-TAI?*

I'D RATHER *FIGHT* THAN HIDE, LORD. ESPECIALLY WITH THESE SIEGE TOWERS IN THE OFFING.

WHO WILL *REPEL* ALL MAGICAL ATTACKS SIMPLY BY HIS PRESENCE.

BUT I SHARE YOUR INSTINCTS. *HASHARITO*, RISE AND APPROACH US.

I AM YOURS TO *COMMAND,* LORD.

YOU WILL RIDE IN OUR *VANGUARD* AND KILL THE KONDOBU, *KAIKOU HARA.* HE WHO BEARS YOUR FACE.

BUT--IF WE MEET *KUMORI-RINJIN* IN THE FIELD, WE HAVE TO FACE THE *KONDOBU.*

ONLY THEN CAN OUR *SPELL-BOOKS* BE UNLOCKED AND UNLEASHED.

I *OBEY,* LORD.

YOU *FAILED* ME ONCE IN THIS, REMEMBER. YOU MUST NOT *HESITATE* OR GIVE HIM QUARTER.

MASTER!

WHY WOULD I DO *THAT?*

IS THERE A GOOD PLACE FOR AN *AMBUSH* CLOSE TO THE FORTRESS, MUMBU-TAI?

THERE IS A *PERFECT* PLACE. THE *GORGE OF QAN.*

LOTS OF *LEDGES* FOR ARCHERS. LOTS OF NATURAL *COVER.*

OF COURSE, PERFECT SPOTS ARE DOUBLE-EDGED *SWORDS.*

THE *ENEMY* TENDS TO SEE THEM TOO, UNLESS HE'S A *HALF-WIT.*

THEN LET'S GIVE THE SHADOW-DRAGON THE BENEFIT OF THE *DOUBT--*

--AND *PLAN* ACCORDINGLY.

SO, LORD *ASIRO-SAMIRO*--

--THIS IS WAR.

IT WAS ONE OF YOUR FAVORITE *OCCUPATIONS* IN TIMES PAST.

DOES THE SIGHT OF IT STRIKE A *CHORD?*

SO MANY SWORDS. I REMEMBER...

...A THOUSAND, THOUSAND SWORDS. AND THEN *ONE*. ONE ONLY.

AIDONO. THE ALTAR. LORD ARATSU'S BLADE, THAT CUTS AWAY PAST AND FUTURE.

IT IS A FEARSOME WEAPON.

YOU SEEM TROUBLED, MASTER RA. ARE YOU HAVING ECOND THOUGHTS ABOUT OUR STRATEGY?

NO. BUT I'M NO FIGHTER, LORD RINJIN.

I DON'T KNOW IF I CAN DO ANY OF THIS.

DO YOU KNOW THE ORIGAMI SCULPTURE CALLED THE DRAGON?

NO.

IT IS EXTREMELY INTRICATE.

AND IN MAKING IT YOU MUST PASS THROUGH MANY INTERMEDIATE FORMS.

SOME OF THESE TRANSITIONAL STAGES ARE VERY BEAUTIFUL. THEY LOOK LIKE END POINTS IN THEIR OWN RIGHT.

THE SEATED MAN. THE ROSE. THE OPEN HAND.

I APOLOGIZE OR THE LABORED ANALOGY.

BUT LIFE FOLDS EACH OF US INTO MANY CURIOUS SHAPES BEFORE WE FINALLY BECOME WHAT WE ARE MEANT TO BE.

EXALTED ONE, YOU ASKED FOR THE KONDOBU'S ARMOR TO BE BROUGHT TO YOU.

INDEED I DID.

TIME TO SILENCE YOUR DOUBTS, KAIKOU--

--AND BECOME THE DRAGON.

LORETTA, ARE YOU GOING TO *SKULK* IN YOUR *ROOM* ALL DAY?

THAT'S A *TERRIBLE* WAY FOR A GIRL YOUR AGE TO TALK.

YOU CAN'T CARRY ON LIKE THIS, LORETTA. I *MEAN* IT.

PROBABLY NOT.

IN ANOTHER HOUR OR SO I'LL GO TO *SCHOOL*, SIGN THE LATES REGISTER AND GO SKULK BEHIND THE *GYM*.

NO.

I *CAN'T*, CAN I?

THE **GORGE OF QAN,** MY LORD.

YOU ASKED TO BE TOLD WHEN WE REACHED THIS POINT.

BUT--THE KONDOBU WHEELS **LEFT,** TOWARDS HINSO-BASHO **INSTEAD.**

THEN THAT'S WHERE OUR WAY LIES, ACROSS THE **LAKE.**

GIVE THE ORDER, SABURO.

I LIKE NOT TO FOLLOW SOME STRIPLING **BOY,** TSELI.

A **KONDOBU.**

KONDOBU OR NOT, HE'S NO **BEARD** AND HIS VOICE PIPES LIKE A **GIRL'S.**

AND TO MARCH AROUND THE **LAKE** WILL TAKE US THREE HOURS OUT OF OUR WAY.

LORD RINJIN'S ORDERS WERE **PRECISE,** FRIEND IRAKO, AND CLEAR.

WE MARCH **ACROSS** HINSO-BASHO, NOT **AROUND** IT.

KRESCHHHHH

TUNNNNNG
TUNNNNNG
TUNNNNNG

HOLD YOUR RANKS, CURSE YOU!

HOLD YOUR RANKS!

SOLDIERS, YOUR TARGETS ARE THE SIEGE TOWERS AND THE TREBUCHETS. FOR THE HONOR OF THE SWORD-KING--

--CHAAAARGE!

BRING PITCH AND *TINDER,* KAO-FENG.

WE'LL *BURN* THESE TOWERS--

KLUDD

--AND WARM OUR HANDS AT THE BLAZE.

SHRIPPPP

M-MASTER MUMBU-TAI, I--

--I THINK--

THIS IS NO *SIEGE* ENGINE.

IT'S PAINTED *CANVAS.*

AH AH AH AH

YOU WERE *GOOD*, ASSASSIN.

I'LL *GIVE* YOU THAT.

YOU JUST--

--DIDN'T REALLY KEEP YOUR *MIND* ON THE JOB.

MY MASTER ASKED TO SEE YOUR *HEAD*.

I HOPE YOU DON'T OBJECT. YOU DON'T SEEM TO HAVE ANY FURTHER *USE* FOR--

...

SO I AM-- *REDEEMED*--TOSHI HARA.

AND YOU--

--YOU ARE--

NURRHH!

KA-TESCHHHHH.

OR THE SULT.

AHHRRR!

COME, HARA. YOU WANTED TO **MEASURE** YOUR-SELF AGAINST ME.

IT'S TOO **LATE** NOW TO CHANGE YOUR MIND.

I **HAVEN'T**-- CHANGED MY MIND. YOU TRIED TO DESTROY--MY **FAMILY.**

AND NOW-- I'M GOING TO **KILL** YOU.

LORD RINJIN, WE MUST FALL BACK. ARATSU'S *SPELL-BOOKS* HAVE WON THE DAY FOR HIM!

HOLD THE *LINE*, SUMASHI.

BUT WE HAVE *NOTHING!* NO DEFENSE!

DEFENSE? WE ARE ABOUT TO *ATTACK.*

KESCHHH

GUUUH!

TISCHHH

AND NOW WE ARE DONE. YOU HAVE *COURAGE,* BOY, BUT YOU LACK FORESIGHT.

TO COME AGAINST ME WITH *BLADES,* WHEN YOU KNOW NO BLADE WILL *DISRESPECT* ME ENOUGH TO TOUCH ME.

ACTUALLY--LORD ARATSU--

--I'VE BEEN LUCKY ENOUGH--

--TO MEET *TWO.*

BUT *ONE* IS ALL IT TAKES.

"THE *LOYAL* SERVANT.

"THE GREAT *DETECTIVE.*

"THE *EXILE--*"

Y-- Y-- --YAMADA--?

YOU MUST KEEP MOVING, KAIKOU. YOU MUST FIND THE SWORD.

THE SWORD THAT STEALS THE PAST.

HUH — HUH — HUH

YAMADA, IS THIS THE ONE? IS THIS *AIDONO?*

I DO NOT THINK SO, KAIKOU. HE KEEPS *THAT* BLADE IN HIS AUDIENCE CHAMBER.

BESIDE THE *CHAIR* IN WHICH HE SITS.

TELL ME-- THE WAY.

HUH.

AND KEEP ME *MOVING*--IF I STOP.

...

VERY *CLEVER.*

T-TOSHI!

ALL OF IT. I'M REALLY IMPRESSED.

TOSHI, THAT SWORD. IT'S--IT'S THE ONE THAT TOOK YOUR *MEMORIES* AWAY.

GIVE IT-- TO ME, AND I CAN--

GIVE YOU A *WEAPON?* WHAT AN INTERESTING SUGGESTION.

I C--CAN TAKE AWAY ITS *POWER,* WITH MY TOUCH. *CURE* YOU.

OF COURSE.

JUST LET ME--*TOUCH* IT.

WELL--

--PERHAPS I *WILL.*

切恋愛
EXTREME LOVE!!!

STARRING
MIMI
OGUNO

"TIME."

IT DOESN'T WORK, DOES IT?

IN WHAT SENSE?

IT'S SUPPOSED TO MAKE EVERYTHING *OKAY* AGAIN, ISN'T IT?

THE *BOMB* DROPS, THEN EVERYONE MAKES FRIENDS AND WE BUILD A *PEACE PARK.* LIFE GOES ON.

BUT WE SAW *GRANITE* TURN INTO STEAM, DIDN'T WE, *SABURO?* SO WE KNOW. TIME ISN'T A RIVER, ITS A *KNIFE.*

I DON'T THINK I UNDERSTAND YOUR *REFERENCE.*

HER MAJESTY WANTS TO KNOW IF YOUR *AFFAIRS* ARE SETTLED.

EVERYTHING TURNS ON A MOMENT. LIVES AND *DIES* IN A MOMENT. THAT'S WHAT MY MOM AND DAD NEVER *TOLD* ME.

WHAT DOES THAT EVEN *MEAN?*

IT MEANS, ARE YOU *TIED* TO ANYTHING HERE?

WILL THERE BE ANYTHING TO *DISTRACT* YOU OR GIVE YOU PAUSE?

"I BROUGHT HIM *HOME,* AND WE HAD A FUNERAL.

"IT SEEMED LIKE THE RIGHT THING TO *DO.*

"AND I WENT BACK TO TOKYO, TO SEE THAT *GIRL* HE HUNG OUT WITH.

"I GAVE HER THE DAGGER. IT SAID IT *KNEW* HER, AND COULD EXPLAIN WHAT HAPPENED TO KAI BETTER THAN *I* COULD.

"I WENT BACK TO SCHOOL. PRETENDED I HAD A *LIFE* HERE.

"I MEAN--ONE THAT MADE SOME KIND OF *SENSE.*

"BUT I *DREAMED* ABOUT HIM EVERY NIGHT.

"AND I WOKE TO THE HOWLING OF A *GHOST-DOG* THAT NOBODY ELSE COULD HEAR."

SO I CUT OUT MY PARENTS' *MEMORIES* WITH USO-TSUKI.

THEY THINK THEY WERE ALWAYS *CHILDLESS.*

I'M READY TO *GO* WITH YOU-- TO DO WHATEVER IT *TAKES* TO GET HIM BACK.

MY MISTRESS KNOWS WHERE SUCH *SOULS* ARE STORED. BUT SHE MAKES NO *PROMISES.*

I'M NOT *ASKING* FOR ANY.

BUT I LEARN QUICKLY. AND I'M *WORTH* MY HIRE.

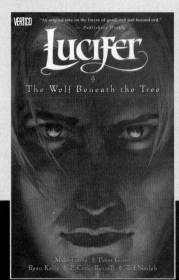